A Christmas on

THE OTHER SIDE OF HEAVEN

JOHN H. GROBERG

DESERET
BOOK

SALT LAKE CITY, UTAH

This account appeared originally in John H. Groberg, *In the Eye of the Storm* (Salt Lake City: Bookcraft, 1993), 236–40. Used by permission.

ISBN 1-59038-352-4

Printed in the United States of America   72076
Publishers Printing, Salt Lake City, Utah

10   9   8   7   6   5   4   3   2   1

December is the warmest time of the year in Tonga, where I spent three Christmases as a young missionary in the 1950s. Despite the hot, humid weather, the Christmas spirit is beautiful. Thinking of Jesus brings great joy. What a blessing it is when people think more about others and less about themselves!

There was not a lot of physical gift-giving in Tonga, as there was not a lot of things to give. People were poor in terms of worldly possessions, but they gave marvelous gifts of love, service, and kindness. During the warm evenings around Christmas, many singing groups and bands went around serenading. Even with the oppressive heat, the feeling of peace and good cheer seemed to permeate everything.

A few months before Christmas one year we were asked to raise £500 so we could start building a new brick chapel in Pangai. We made an assessment of £50 each to ten families, with the request that they have the money in by January 1. Most of the families had completed their allotment by early December, but one older couple was still struggling. They were a faithful grandparent couple whose children were all married and gone.

The grandfather originally had some sources in mind from which he could get the money, but one by one those sources failed, and he realized he would need to go to his plantation on another island to make copra to sell. (Copra is used commercially for soaps and oils.) Making copra involved gathering coconuts, cutting them open, extracting the meat, and drying it in the sun before selling it to the *mataka* (copra board). He was determined to get the needed money by the January 1 deadline, so two weeks before Christmas he left for his plantation.

Shortly afterward, a nine-year-old granddaughter came from Tongatapu to spend the holidays. Her arrival was unannounced but welcomed by her grandmother.

The grandmother and her granddaughter had a good time together. Then a few days before Christmas, the granddaughter became very ill with a high fever. Even though her grandmother put her to bed and cared for her well, the fever seemed to get worse. The grandmother asked my companion and me to administer to the girl, which we did. I felt she would be all right, and we continued about our other activities.

The day before Christmas, we visited several families to wish them the season's best. As we concluded our visits, I asked my companion where else he thought we should go that Christmas Eve. He replied, "I've heard that the granddaughter is still doing poorly and that the grandfather has not yet returned. I'm sure the grandmother is very tired from the constant care she has been giving her granddaughter. Why don't we go to her house and volunteer to watch her granddaughter tonight and let her get some rest?"

What a great idea! I thought. *Why don't I think of things like that?*

It was early evening when we arrived at the grandmother's house and explained what we proposed to do. Seldom have I seen more grateful eyes or felt more sincere appreciation. The grandmother looked at us a long time, probably studying our seriousness, and then said, "She is very ill. I have been up day and night with her for the last three days. I am very tired, and I'm not sure I can make it another night. Thank you. Thank you! I have been using this cloth and bowl of water to cool her brow and this woven fan to give her some air movement. She has not talked at all the last few days, only moaned. I'm not sure if she will get well or not. Maybe I should try to stay up and help."

My companion said, "No, you go and rest. *Kolipoki* (my Tongan name) and I will fan her and cool her forehead, and she will be all right. Now run along and sleep." She looked at us again for a long time and then left. I imagine she was asleep the second she lay down.

We were on the front veranda of the house, where it was a little cooler than inside. We immediately started fanning the granddaughter and cooling her forehead with the wet cloth. She seemed in a bad way. Her breathing was strange, her fever was high, her eyes were closed, and her moans were pathetic. We devised a system whereby one would hold the wet cloth and the other would fan the air through it to get some cool air moving around the girl's mouth and head.

It doesn't sound like much work, but the anxiety of the situation, the sultry evening, and the exertion to get water, rinse the cloth, and constantly wave the fan caused us both to tire quickly. I appreciated the grandmother and her constant care more than ever.

At around eleven o'clock we realized we must do something different to make it through the night, as we were both very tired. My companion again came up with an idea. "Why don't we take turns?" he said. "You sleep for an hour while I care for her, then I'll wake you and you care for her an hour while I sleep, then you wake me, and so on. At least we'll get through the night that way."

"Fine," I said. "Who should start?"

"I'll start," he replied. "You rest first." So I lay down to sleep, and he cared for the child alone. At midnight he woke me, and I fanned with one hand and sponged her forehead with the other until one o'clock, when I woke him. He woke me at two, and I, in turn, woke him at three. I knew he would wake me for my next turn at four o'clock. Even though I was very tired, I knew this was fair.

The next thing I knew, sunlight was streaming into my eyes. I awakened, jumped up, and said, "What time is it?"

"It's six o'clock," my companion replied.

"Six o'clock! You were supposed to get me up at four! Why didn't you wake me?" I asked.

He had a broad smile on his face, which was intensified by the bright rays of the early morning sun. That smile seemed to come from deep within his soul; it encompassed his whole being as he replied, "Oh, you looked so tired. I decided to let you sleep. It's my present to you. Merry Christmas!"

I couldn't say anything. I just looked at him in admiration and wondered, *Why don't I think of things like that? My companion is a great man. God loves him. He stayed up for me. Why am I so weak?* I thought of the Savior coming to his sleeping disciples and asking, "Could ye not watch with me one hour?" (Matthew 26:40). The Savior stayed up most of the night performing the greatest work of love in the world while those close to him slept. Yet, as he returned and saw them sleeping again, he merely looked at them and quietly said, "Sleep on" (v. 45).

I felt ashamed, yet I also felt happy as I saw the joy in my companion's face. His radiant smile was almost angelic.

Sometime during those early morning hours the girl's moaning ceased and her fever broke. She stirred and opened her eyes. Although she was still very weak, we knew she would be all right. We waited till midmorning to knock on the door to wake the grandmother. She answered the knock quickly, possibly expecting the worst. When she came out on the porch, her granddaughter was sitting up. We were all smiles as we said in unison, "Merry Christmas!" It was good to have her and her granddaughter both feeling so much better—a wonderful way to start Christmas Day. We had many other things to do, so we left and went about our regular missionary activities.

Over time I largely forgot about this experience until many years later when I was asked to speak at the funeral for my faithful Tongan missionary companion. He had lived a good life and then died of cancer. While speaking in Tongan, I suddenly received a flash of understanding that made a deep and clear impression on me. I emphasize that this was not a vision, a revelation, or a dream but rather a feeling and an understanding wherein I sensed the following:

I saw a beautiful place with throngs of people anxiously waiting to get to a certain area. There was no pushing or shoving but rather a respectful and excited pressing forward to this particular place.

I saw a young man whom I recognized in the throng. He was smiling and patiently moving along with the others when suddenly his name was called. Someone in authority came and took him by the arm and led him past the waiting crowds, directly to the desired area. His guide said a few words to someone who seemed to control the entrance, and this person smiled and ushered the young man through.

Everyone in the huge crowd seemed to be aware of what had happened. People turned to one another and began to comment, not in anger or jealousy but rather in wonder and happiness for the young man who had gotten to that desirable place so quickly.

The guide came back and began waiting patiently with the throngs of people. Someone leaned over and asked him about the young man. The guide whispered something to him and immediately the questioner's face lit up with a deep smile. He nodded his head approvingly and turned and told his neighbor. Almost instantly everyone seemed to know the answer. I strained to understand and finally heard someone say, "Oh, he let his companion sleep when he was very tired."

I offer no more explanation than what I have related. I learned that deeds of sacrifice, deeds of selflessness and honesty, deeds of effort in sincerely trying to help others, especially at the expense of one's own comfort (in essence the true spirit of Christmas), never go unnoticed by the powers of heaven.